Angels On Tap

Angels On Tap

For information, address:

BearManor Media
P. O. Box 71426
Albany, GA 31708

bearmanormedia.com

Typesetting and layout by John Teehan

Published in the USA by BearManor Media

ISBN—978-1-62933-124-9

Angels On Tap

by
Burt Prelutsky

BearManor Media

2017

This book, like my life, is dedicated to my wife, Yvonne, who proves that the third time really is the charm.

CHAPTER I

THE BAR

EVERY REPORTER DREAMS that once in his life a story fraught with drama, suspense and mini-series possibilities, will drop in his lap.

Of course, as with most dreams, a number of circumstances have to magically convene to make it happen. In my case, I'm a good reporter, sure. But, mainly, what I was, was just darn lucky.

In the beginning, I certainly didn't feel lucky. Far from it.

It was dark, it was raining and my car had started burning oil on the freeway. I took the first off-ramp—one I wasn't familiar with—drove around for a few anxious blocks, and then pulled up in front of a bar. It was the only thing in sight with lights on. I figured I'd call the Auto Club and have a cold one while I waited. The place, by the way, was called Gabriel's.

The second I walked through the door, I sensed this wasn't your typical foot-of-the-freeway, hole-in-the-wall, dive. There was, for the lack of a better term, something "other worldly" about the place. At first, it was hard to put my finger on it.

Then, taking a harder look around, it hit me. When you've been a top newspaper reporter as long as I have, it becomes second nature to see things other people could trip over without ever noticing. At Gabriel's, what I spotted was the fact that everyone in the joint, except yours truly, was wearing wings. Well, perhaps "wearing" isn't the right word. You wear a raincoat; you have a nose. These folks had wings.

Now, you might think that would be a rather startling sight. Maybe you're even thinking that you would have noticed it right off the bat, even if you weren't worrying about your car and whether the Club would arrive before the Second Coming and whether there would ever be peace in the Middle East and whether the Red Sox have the pitching to carry them through July for a change. In any case, the thing you have to remember is that everyone in the room—bartender and customers alike—had wings. Under those circumstances, it just might not be as obvious as you think. When enough people are doing something—be it the wave or voting for Bernie Sanders—it's just not as startling as you might think.

Anyway, there I was, standing in the middle of Gabriel's, nursing a root beer, noticing all these wings, but trying to play it cool. Which definitely wasn't easy. I mean, we've all seen wings, but they've always come attached to birds, planes and hospitals. But, believe me, seeing them on a roomful of people is quite another matter. You don't want to be rude and stare. But you sure can't help peeking. Which, I'm afraid, is what I was doing when a voice called out from behind the bar.

Before I could respond, the bartender came over and shook hands. "Hi," he said, "I'm Gabriel. We don't get too many civilians in here. You must have *really* gotten lost."

"I guess so. I'm not dead, am I?"

"No," he laughed, "we are."

"Oh. I just thought that might explain why I'm suddenly seeing angels."

"Oh, lots of people see angels, but it's usually one at a time."

I could tell I was on to something. This had Pulitzer Prize written all over it.

Gabriel topped off my root beer. "You're a reporter, aren't you?"

"How would you know that?"

"You'd be surprised what we know. For instance, give me a year and I'll tell you what it's famous for."

"Okay. How about 1513?"

"Nothing."

"You don't remember 1513?"

"I remember it, but nothing memorable happened. It was a lot like 762. Every once in a while, a year comes along that's so boring, the best thing you can do is lie down and take a nap 'til it's over."

"I know what you mean. I felt that way about 1987."

"Yeah, that was a snooze. Ask me about 1398."

"What about 1398?"

"Jan Hus was lecturing on theology at Prague University."

"That made it memorable?"

"Yes, because Jan Hus was the most boring public speaker who ever lived. Ten minutes into a speech, he could put 500 people to sleep. When he rehearsed his talks at home, his dog would fall asleep. When he practiced outdoors, horses and cows would doze off. Birds would fall out of the trees."

"Gee, and I thought Bill Maher was bad."

Frankly, I didn't know what to think. Was I losing my mind? Should I write all this down or should I run out of the place screaming like a banshee? I, being a rational human being, was inclined to run and scream. But I, the intrepid newshound, opted to stay. Like young Pip, I was a gentleman with great expectations. The Pulitzer was only the beginning.

My brain was feverish with sugar plum possibilities. There were visions of book deals, the corner table at Elaine's, one-on-one's with Diane Sawyer, Johnny Depp portraying me in "Angel Man," photo-ops with Donald and Melania.

Still, I couldn't figure it out. If the bar had been around a while, wouldn't someone else have beaten me to the story? When I raised the question, Gabriel simply rolled his eyes. Although he was too polite to call me a schnook to my face, there was schnook written all over his expression.

"You're not the first writer to stop by," he replied.

"I'm not?"

"Nope. A lot of guys gave it a shot, but nothing's ever been published. Shelley tried it as a sonnet; Homer, a Greek tragedy. I'll tell you what I told them—it's just a bar. It's a bar like any other bar, except that all the customers are angels. Which means they have wings, but no pockets. So, don't expect a lot of tips."

"You're making my mouth water," I had to confess.

"I can see that," Gabriel said, handing me a napkin.

"It's a story that has to be written."

"But, nobody's going to publish it. They're going to laugh at you, son. They're going to say it's unbelievable."

"They published *The Bridges of Madison County*," I reminded him. "Anything's possible."

At that moment, someone dropped a glass. It sounded so much like a gun shot, I jumped two feet in the air. "No reason to be scared," Gabriel assured me. "Around here, we like to say that every time someone breaks a whiskey glass, an angel gets his wings."

That was the beginning of the story that changed my life. On the spot, I decided to interview the flock of them. (Flock happens to be the appropriate word, I discovered. It's pride of lions, den of thieves, flock of angels, in case you ever wake up one day and find yourself on "Jeopardy".)

In short order, I commandeered a corner table and let the angels know that the drinks were on me so long as I got my questions answered. Basically, I wanted to find out who they were, what they did and whether, for the most part, angeling was a good job. What follows is a verbatim transcript of the interviews I conducted that unforgettable night at Gabriel's.

Let the world judge.

– Burt Prelutsky

CHAPTER II

THE ANGEL HORACE

MY FIRST SUBJECT WAS A ROLY-POLY gentleman with red cheeks and a gap between his front teeth. He looked like he was born to play Santa Claus. Of course, for all I knew, he *was* Santa Claus. It was, after all, turning out to be that sort of night.

Q. How does one become an angel?

A: Well, in the old days, God just created them. Out of whole cloth, as it were. But, as people started begatting all over the place, the angels couldn't keep up. So, God solved the problem by appointing human beings.

Q. Dead ones?

A. Yes, that is the one prerequisite.

Q. So, what's the procedure?

A. First you die. Then, after your papers are processed, you get your assignment.

Q. What sort of assignments do you get?

A. Most of us are supposed to look after people, but only within specific areas.

Q. So, you're all specialists?

A. Exactly. It wasn't always this way, of course. Way back then, when life was simpler, we were all general practitioners. Back then, there was only so much trouble people could get into. So long as they didn't get mixed up with witches and remembered to pray thirty or forty times a day, the job was a snap.

Q. What did it consist of?

A. For the most part, hovering.

Q. Hovering?

A. You've seen the old paintings. It was like that. We hovered a lot. Every time someone important was born, we were there, hovering overhead. Likewise, when they died. We'd also show up at weddings, crucifixions and most of your bigger shindigs.

Q. So, what changed?

A. Things started going downhill when people began moving to town. Once they left the farm, they started getting fancy ideas. Before you knew it, they stopped putting us in all the pictures. Suddenly, no more hovering angels. Overnight, you couldn't unload a painting with an angel if you were giving away free dishes with it. Pussy cats on velvet, children with eyes the size of salad bowls, seven dogs wearing derbies and playing poker—that's what people were buying. Phooey, feh!

Q. What's it like being an angel?

A. It's a job.

Q. Is it like being alive, though?

A. In some ways, it's better.

Q. Oh, really?

A. Sure. For one thing, we don't have to punch a clock. There are no union dues, no lock-outs and we never go on strike.

Q. In what ways is it worse?

A. No paid vacations, no bad-mouthing management and, as far as retirement goes, forget it!

Q. You never get to retire? Can't you complain to anyone?

A. Of course, it's a God-given right to gripe. Unfortunately, it's also a right that God reserves for Himself. And you should hear Him when He gets started! You'd think nothing ever turned out the way He planned.

Q. Really? Like what?

A. You name it.

Q. Okay...sex.

A. Big mistake, total accident. Satan blindsided Him on that one, and He's never gotten over it.

Q. How did God expect people to reproduce without sex? I mean, let's face facts, Horace, without it, Adam would have been the first man and the last man. Surely God didn't intend for the human race to be a mere footnote in the history of the universe.

A. Well, yes, actually He did.

Q. He did?!

A. Yeah. But if you ever run into Him, don't bring it up. Learn from my bitter experience and don't get Him started.

Q. Tell me, Horace, what's the best thing about being an angel?

A. You can sneak into movies for free.

Q. What's the worst thing?

A. The movies.

I asked Horace if he thought his fellow angels would agree to be interviewed.

A. I don't see why not. They've talked to all the others.

Q. I heard about Shelley and Homer. Who were the others?

A. Shakespeare, Milton, Twain, Melville, Tolstoy, Poe, Hemingway, Spillane, they've all stopped by.

Q. Shakespeare?

A. At this very table. Or was it Bacon? It was one of those two-plume guys.

Q. Two plumes?

A. Yeah, one for wearing, one for writing.

Q. Twain, Melville? I can't believe they've all been here.

A. That's the problem. Nobody could believe it. They all wrote about us, but they couldn't get the stuff published. And you won't be able to, either

Q. Don't be too sure about that.

A. Hey, if William Shakespeare and Mickey Spillane struck out, what chance do you have?

Q. People are a lot more open today, a lot more broad-minded and accepting of things they can't see.

A. Do you mean, gullible?

Q. I do not. I just mean that there's a lot more interest in spiritual things these days. People are ready, even eager, to believe in the unbelievable.

A. You really think so?

Q. Absolutely.

A. What a rotten shame!

Q. Why do you say that? I thought you'd be overjoyed to know that there's a world out there waiting to hear your story.

A. Overjoyed? Are you kidding? You seem like a nice guy and all, but we could have had Jane Austen and wound up with our own English mini-series! Instead, we wind up with you, a fellow without a plume.

CHAPTER III

THE ANGEL HELEN

WITH THAT, HORACE STOOD UP and returned to his stool. And not a minute too soon. His place at my booth was taken by a very attractive female angel. At least she would have been very attractive if the pain had been absent from her eyes. Think Deborah Kerr in *From Here to Eternity*.

She slid in across from me, offered her hand, which I shook, and her name, which I wrote down. The name I wrote was Helen.

Q. According to Horace, each of you has a specific area of responsibility. What's yours?

A. I'd rather not say.

I must confess that took me aback. I thought maybe she was pulling my leg. But, I checked and she wasn't. A lesser man might have quit right there and written up the Horace interview for the Reader's Digest. You know, the Most Unforgettable Angel I Ever Met. But, I had a hunch I was on to something bigger than that.

Besides, we members of the media are a notoriously thick-skinned lot. And nothing short of a stake in the heart will stop us when we're on the trail of a scoop or, at a P.R. shindig, when they're passing out those little pigs-in-a-blanket on a first-come, first-served, basis. A cattle stampede can't hold a candle.

Q. Why don't you want to tell me?

A. It's embarrassing.

Q. Okay, fair's fair. How about if I tell you something embarrassing about myself? Then, it'll be your turn. My middle name is Beagle. My mother raised them.

A. Well, you're right, Beagle boy, compared to that, my secret's pretty puny stuff. I'm responsible for the fine arts.

Q. What's so awful about that?

A. Just look around you. In the blink of an eye, the world has gone from Bach and Beethoven to hip-hop and rap. We've gone from Rembrandt and Da Vinci to Pop Art and graffiti. Think how that reflects on me. How would you feel if everyone blamed you for the fall of Western Civilization?

Q. If it has you so upset, why didn't you do something about it? You can call it the blink of an eye if it makes you feel any better, but that was a pretty long blink between *Hamlet* and *Home Alone 2*. Where were you, anyway? On the world's longest coffee break? Off at the beach, trying to wade through *War and Peace*?

A. I am a muse. And, clearly, you are unaware of a muse's role.

Q. So, what happened? Get all mused out?

A. It's you people! You stopped wanting to be divinely inspired. Writers stopped writing great novels and started writing bad movies. Composers lost interest in symphonies and concentrated on jingles selling soap and potato chips. Architects stopped designing cathedrals like Notre Dame and started designing towers like Notre Trump.

Q. I see what you mean.

A. There used to be hundreds of us in the arts department. It was thrilling. More than a mere job, it was a calling. Every time you turned around—voila!—another masterpiece.

Q. What happened?

A. What always happens? Funding for the arts dries up, the usual cutbacks take place, and here I am—Helen, the lone surviving muse.

Q. How can one angel handle the load? You must be exhausted.

A. Far from it. I only wish I were buried in work. Great, noble, inspiring work. It's mother's milk to me. As it is, the last person who actually sought creative inspiration was Andy Warhol, and I'm afraid he misunderstood when I told him that to be a great artist, he might have to survive on Campbell Soup.

Q. I'm amazed that you have to oversee all the fine arts. I'd think painters, alone, would keep you hopping.

A. Hopping mad. Somewhere along the way, the art of painting became the art of framing. People put frames around dots or drips or smudges, and the stuff would sell for millions. Without the fancy frames, they're the sort of things that parents of very young children attach to their refrigerators with little magnets.

Q. Still, I imagine you've met all of the greatest artists who ever lived.

A. I knew them all, except for Roka.

Q. Who was Roka?

A. He was the first one to do cave drawings. By the time I realized it was art and not vandalism, it was too late to meet him.

Q. Why? What happened?

A. A dinosaur ate him for breakfast. And, so, art criticism was born.

Q. Can you tell me about some of the great painters you have known?

A. Well, I hate to drop names, but perhaps you've heard of Michelangelo.

Q. I should say so. I imagine he was the greatest of them all.

A. Certainly the laziest.

Q. How can you say that? A lazy man painted the ceiling of the Sistine Chapel? Surely you jest.

A. He only took the job because he could do it lying down.

Q. Still, it was a tremendous achievement. Didn't it take him four or five years?

A. Of course. That's because he kept napping. Anyone else would have had it finished in two weeks, tops. Frankly, in all honesty, I have to admit I out-did myself that time.

Q. How so?

A. Maybe you think it's easy being museful when, every time you come around, the artist is two hundred feet up in the air, snoring like a bear.

Q. No, I can see where that would be a real challenge. Looking back over your career, who are some of the other artists who stand out?

A. Picasso was almost as cute as he thought he was, Dali was crazy as a poodle, Rembrandt never took a bath,

Whistler was a mama's boy, and the biggest pain in the neck was that Botticelli.

Q. And why was that?

A. He's the one who insisted on painting us angels with those sappy robes and the big halos, the flowing ribbons and all the rest of that silly folderol.

Q. But that's how you look.

A. That's how we have to look because of him. It's how people expect us to look, all because of his goofy pictures. The man wasn't an artist, he was a costume designer with a paint brush. If we showed up, not looking the way he painted us, folks thought we were just ghosts or the end result of too many dry martinis. But, so long as we appeared looking like something whipped up by a French pastry chef, people took us seriously.

Q. And did Botticelli become an angel when he died?

A. Why do you ask?

Q. I just thought it would be very ironic if he, himself, wound up having to spend eternity looking like a slice of wedding cake.

A. Yes, I suppose that would have been ironic. But, I'm afraid, old Botticelli didn't exactly get his wings. What he got were his just deserts.

Q. What happened to him?

A. He's a bellboy at the Hotel Purgatory.

Q. Gee, I bet he wishes he'd stuck to landscapes.

A. Too late now. What he didn't realize, I'm afraid, is that angels don't get irony—they get even.

CHAPTER IV

THE ANGEL WALLY

THE NEXT ANGEL—who would be described as port-ly by a master of understatement—could barely squeeze into the booth.

"Name's Wally," he said, extending a pudgy hand for me to shake. "Food and beverage are my line."

Q. Gee, I never would have guessed Heaven took an interest in that sort of thing.

A. Well, officially, I work in the food and beverage division of the Health Department. That fellow over there by the window, the one running in place, is Sean, the angel of jogging. That woman on the way to the ladies' room is Joyce, the angel of dieting. Ours is one of the few departments that's actually expanding.

Q. What are your duties?

A. Well, let's just say that if not for old Wally, people would still be noshing on twigs, grass and small rodents.

Q. When you put it that way, I guess we all owe you a pretty large debt.

A. I'd say so. Though, actually, field mice were considered delicacies until fairly recently. Heck, fella, it wasn't all that long ago that you folks gobbled up acorns like they were beer nuts.

Q. What changed things?

A. It was decided that there weren't enough differences to distinguish human beings from owls, bears and warthogs, and that, perhaps, diet might be an area worth exploring.

Q. So, it's basically been your responsibility to wean us off bark and onto burgers.

A. It wasn't as easy as it sounds. You people talk about developing a taste for olives and bran flakes, but can you imagine what a time I had trying to convince the very first person to try a lobster? Plus, keep in mind that melted butter hadn't been invented yet.

Q. I bet it was even harder to get us started on snails.

A. That time I just got lucky. Butter or no butter, at the rate those little rascals reproduce, if some French gardener hadn't had a brainstorm and thought of calling them escargots, you'd be buried in them by now.

Q. Not a pretty picture. What have been some of your other major victories?

A. How'd you like to coax someone into trying yogurt before the stuff even had a name?

Q. How'd you manage?

A. I found some poor soul who'd been wandering around lost in the Gobi Desert for two weeks, dining on sand and his sneakers.

Q. Good thinking.

A. And even then, he didn't cave in for another five days.

Q. What has been your single greatest challenge?

A. Artichokes. For the first few thousand years they were around, even I couldn't figure out how to eat them.

Q. Who came up with the idea of eating three meals a day?

A. The English. In the fourteenth century, there were two princes, Harold the Fat and Bertram the Bulimic. Harold felt that five meals a day was just about right, while his brother Bertram argued that one was more than enough. Especially if you didn't swallow. Before war broke out between the two factions, their father, Arnold the Moderate, worked out a compromise. It was also Arnold who gave the meals their names. Breakfast was so called because it broke a fast. Dinner got its name from the bell which they used to ring when it was time to eat.

Q. And lunch?

A. Named after the Duke of Lunch, the man who said, "Just because it's too late for breakfast and too early for dinner, doesn't mean we've got to starve."

Q. Who were some of the great chefs you have known?

A. At the top of the list, Charles of the Ritz, who's famous for his toasted cheese sandwich.

Q. He invented it?

A. No, but he did perfect it. He's the guy who first burnt the cheese around the edge a little. The man was a genius.

Q. Would you agree with those who contend that all the greatest chefs have been men?

A. Of course not. What about Lucretia Borgia?

Q. But, didn't she…?

A. Okay, nobody's perfect. But, put that woman and some rigatoni in the same kitchen, and it was magic.

Q. There are those who insist it's immoral to eat meat. What do you think?

A. My attitude is that if it tastes good, eat it. After all, morality is often a matter of geography. In one place, bugs are pests, in another they're protein. In some countries, dogs are beloved pets, while in others they're the entre. Frankly, I thought it was a giant leap up the evolutionary ladder once people started eating mutton and quit dating it.

Q. One last question, Wally.

A. Shoot.

Q. What can you tell me about the Last Supper?

A. I'll tell you exactly what I told them at the time. White wine with fish, don't overcook the potatoes, and, most important of all, twelve's company, thirteen's a crowd.

CHAPTER V

THE ANGEL HARRY

WALLY'S PLACE WAS QUICKLY TAKEN, if not literally filled, by someone who looked so much like my late uncle Sidney that I wondered if it wasn't him. On his pinkie, he had a ring that sparkled like an iceberg, though I wouldn't swear it could cut glass. He puffed on a cigar that seemed to have been rolled from equal parts tobacco and shag carpet. And, under his breath, I heard him humming *There's No Business Like Show Business*. He looked like he should be wearing a tattersall vest, a derby hat and spats.

"Uncle Sidney?" I ventured.

"I'm afraid not, sonny boy. My handle's Harry. I once knew an Uncle Sidney, but he was my uncle, not yours."

"It's just that you look familiar."

"A lot of people say that. I think I look like Ziegfeld, but taller. And with wings."

Q. What is your job, Harry?

A. Show biz isn't a job, it's my life. Or at least it would be, if I had a life.

Q. What is it you do?

A. What don't I do? I've done it all. And, best of all, I've done it my way

Before he could break into song, I asked what it was exactly that he'd done his way.

A. I invented entertainment. Before me, people knew there was something missing from their lives, but they didn't know what. They'd just sit around for hours at a time, scratching their heads and moaning.

Q. How did you go about inventing entertainment?

A. I organized the women. Every night, I'd get them to go up to their husbands and say, "You never take me anywhere. We never do anything together. All you do is sit on that rock, scratching and moaning." Within a week, Herbie, the first entertainer, was packing 'em in.

Q. Doing what?

A. Herbie used to throw nineteen rocks in the air at one time.

Q. And that's how we got juggling?

A. No, that's how we got dodging and ducking. Juggling came along much later and involved three oranges.

Q. What form of entertainment do you enjoy the most?

A. For my part, you can't beat vaudeville. Dog acts, ventriloquists, tumblers, Irish comics, German comics, dancing sisters, barber shop quartets, the whole razzamatazz. Before then, what you had, mostly, were your wandering troubadours and your court jesters. Give me a dog walks on his hind legs any day.

Q. Court jesters weren't entertaining?

A. They just dressed funny. There were no comedy writers around feeding them material. It was all very glum.

Q. Who was the first professional comedian?

A. The very first one was Henny Youngfellow. But, he had a short career. Every other line out of his mouth was, "Taketh my wife—prithee."

Q. Well, I guess you live and learn. I've always heard that court jesters actually lived by their wits.

A. In a manner of speaking they did. You see, their main job was to fall down laughing every time the king told a joke. The louder they laughed, the longer they lived. That's where people got the idea that laughter was good for their health.

Q. Weren't any of the jesters funny?

A. Some laughed funnier than others, but even the jester known as Haggas the Hilarious never came up with a better line than "That's no Lady, that's Lord Ashford's wife!"

Q. You say you were a big fan of vaudeville, but you let it die. Why?

A. Who would have guessed you people would fall for the movies in such a big way? I figured it was a novelty, a fad, like the yo-yo. I thought once Mary Pickford hung up her curls, the whole thing would just blow over. It seems like just yesterday that, for a nickel, you'd see eight acts that would knock your hat off, not to mention chorus girls with some meat on their bones. And today, for eight bucks, you get two hours of Seth Rogen farting and Jim Carrey making faces.

Q. Tell me, who thought up applause?

A. Nobody thought it up. It was just an accident. In the beginning, when people liked a performer, they kept very quiet. The more they liked him, the quieter they were. But, one night, a fellow was making music with rocks, and the mosquitoes were driving everybody nuts. The audience made such a racket slapping themselves, you couldn't hear the music. So, the musician just kept playing. At one fell swoop, rock, applause and encores were introduced.

Q. What do you think of the television medium?

A. In the words of Archangel Fred Allen, they call it a medium because it's never well done.

Q. What forms of entertainment are most popular in Heaven?

A. Pretty much what you'd expect—harp recitals, celestial choirs and *I Love Lucy* reruns.

Q. Obviously, you've seen them all. Who would you say is the greatest entertainer who ever lived?

A. There's no way you can name just one person. After all, could Will Rogers play the musical saw? Could Fanny Brice juggle? If Gallagher and Shean ever tap-danced, I missed it. Could Sally Rand do impressions? Who cares? She was one hot tomato! But, if you're asking me who was the loudest singer, I'm telling you it was Caruso. The man had lungs the size of watermelons. On the other hand, Caruso couldn't whistle. Every time he tried, he sounded like he had crackers in his mouth. Probably why the man never owned a dog. You could look it up. Now, if it was whistling you wanted, you either had to hire Wedemeyer's Birds or sign up Al Jolson. And then it was a toss-up; Jolson had more range, but the birds were housebroken.

Q. I know you don't care for the movies very much, but, in your opinion, who was the greatest of them all? Garbo? Tracy? Gable? Hepburn?

A. Only one of the bunch who ever impressed me was Esther Williams.

Q. Esther Williams?!

A. Who else? The woman was a major star and never once got out of the pool. You think that was easy? You ever try giving a performance in eight feet of water? The chlorine alone could kill you.

Q. And that made her greater than, say, Sir Laurence Olivier?

A. There was no comparison. He acted in the West End, you noticed, but never in the deep end.

CHAPTER VI

THE ANGEL MINERVA

THE LITTLE OLD LADY who sat down across from me looked like Central Casting's idea of everybody's maiden aunt. She wore a plain black dress, probably Size Two unless there's something smaller, with a white lace collar, and little black lace gloves. She probably weighed all of eighty pounds, dripping wet. She looked like she belonged under glass at some doll museum. She had that old lady smell about her that I guess is part talcum, part parchment. And with her sweet old lady smile, she could have been the poster girl for AARP.

I immediately assumed she oversaw retirement communities or nursing home facilities.

I couldn't have been further off the mark if I'd been Donald Trump's barber.

To my opening query, she replied, "My name's Minerva, young man, and my field of expertise, if I might call it that without appearing immodest, is athletics."

"I never would have guessed."

"Well, bless your heart. Actually, I am relatively new to the job. Formerly, I was in charge of what used to be known as the social graces. But, there had been less and less call for my services until, finally, I was as redundant as an appendix."

Q, What happened?

A. I was hoping you could tell me. All I know is that etiquette used to be quite important, and then, one day, it wasn't.

Q. I suppose people simply decided it didn't really make that much difference which fork they used.

A. Actually, the tricky part was getting people to use forks in the first place for something besides scratching their backs.

Q. But, why were the rules of etiquette so elaborate?

A. So that people could relax, knowing exactly how to behave in all social situations. It made certain people comfortable to know how to conform and it made other people just as comfortable knowing how *not* to conform. The problem nowadays, from my vantage point at least, is that there seem to be no rules whatsoever, so everyone is equally off balance. Conformists and non-conformists, alike, keep tripping over each other. But, enough wailing at the bar, as it were. I wouldn't want to be thought guilty of sour grapes. I am quite satisfied with my current position.

Q. Just how was it decided that you, of all angels, would be assigned to sports?

A. I couldn't say for certain, but I would venture that they looked around for something else that had lots of rules governing conduct. Rules, after all, are my meat.

Q. Do you oversee all areas of athletics? Even football and basketball?

A. Oh, then you can still distinguish between the two? You really must be paying close attention. To answer your question, though, basically all physical activity, aside from sex and channel surfing, falls within my domain.

Q. I'm not questioning your qualifications, but.... well, I guess I am questioning your qualifications. You just don't strike me as a jock.

A. Well, I suppose that's why I got the job. They were looking for a civilizing influence. In the old days, after all, things were pretty brutal. With the Mayans, losing athletes were sacrificed to appease the—you should excuse the expression—gods. These days, the worst that happens is they get traded to San Diego.

Q. Do you have a favorite sport?

A. Professional wrestling. Nobody gets hurt.

Q. Are there any sports played in Heaven?

A. Golf is very popular.

Q. Why do you think that is?

A. Maybe because there are no sand traps, no water hazards, and prayers tend to get answered.

Q. What's the strangest sport you've ever seen?

A. Without a doubt, that would have to be early water polo.

Q. Really? Why's that?

A. It took them a while to figure out it just wouldn't work with horses.

Q. Which sport was the worst?

A. Christians versus the lions. Even the bookies didn't care much for that one.

Q. There are those who feel that winning is everything. Are you one of those people?

A. Hardly. I'm firmly of the opinion that the important thing isn't whether you win or lose, but how you play the game. Unless, of course, you happened to be an ancient Mayan.

Q. Do you agree with those who believe that sports are the best way to turn boys into men?

A. Not really. I realize I'm just a little old lady angel, but I've always been surprised that nobody seems to give a second thought to twenty or thirty sweaty young men taking showers together when everyone knows that three or four of them only joined up for that very reason.

CHAPTER VII

THE ANGEL SWIFTY

ANYONE COULD SEE THAT my next subject was trying to drown his sorrow or possibly himself at the rate he was downing shots of rye. It was as if he was finishing up the work begun decades ago by Carrie Nation and Billy Sunday. But instead of waging war on booze by shutting down distilleries or using an axe to turn bar tops into kindling, he looked as if he was on a one-man mission to personally deplete the existing stock.

Q. Pardon me, but could I ask you a few questions?

A. Depends what they are.

Q. We could start with your name.

A. Aloysius J. O'Malley, but my friends call me Swifty. At least they used to when I still had friends.

Q. They died?

A. They did.

Q. Any of them here?

A. I'm afraid not. None of the boys made it. Frankly, I'm kind of surprised I got through. I guess the fact that I was never elected to public office helped.

Q. You were a politician?

A. No, you could say I was an arranger. I arranged for other guys to get elected.

Q. And now?

A. My official duties are to oversee politics, but mainly what I do is overlook.

Q. Overlook?

A. Being an angel, I'm supposed to guide them. The job description says I'm supposed to encourage them to do the right thing. To respect the office and be the servant of the people. Have you ever heard such flapdoodle in your entire life?

Q. Well, I think we all want to have representatives in Congress and the White House we can respect and look up to.

I got the distinct impression he was looking at me as if I were a specimen on a slide and he was studying me under a microscope.

A. Sonny boy, the only time anyone should look up to a politician is when he's hanging from the gallows. I'll hang in there as long as I can drink on the job. I do long for the good old days, though, when the professionals ran things.

Q. Surely you're not saying that the days when Tammany Hall and other big city machines made all the decisions was better.

A. You don't know what you're talking about. These days, the people have to bribe the politicians if they want to get anything done. In those days, the politicians bribed the people. Two dollars if you voted the right way. A real go-getter could make ten bucks on Election Day, and back then ten bucks could feed a family of four for a week.

Q. I find it hard to believe that men like Washington, Jefferson and Madison, would have gone along with you.

A. None of them ever hired the services of Swifty O'Malley, so their opinion and ten cents will get you a ride on the trolley. Today, you have all those boring debates. Then you have endless primaries just to get to the finals. Before the amateurs decided they knew better, the pros went into a smoke-filled room, wheeled and dealed, made a few trades…

Q. Trades?

A. Yeah, I'll trade you the Postmaster General and a seat on the Supreme Court for a Secretary of the Interior and Ambassador to Latvia, and when they came out of the smoky room, you knew which two mugs were going to duke it out in November and you could get your bets down.

Q. That's a pretty cynical attitude. Don't you think any politicians are honest?

A. They can't afford to be even if they happen to be that ill-suited to their chosen profession. Do you know how much it costs to be elected to even a minor office these days?

Q. Not exactly.

A. The last election I worked on was a guy running for the state assembly in New Jersey. For the same money, he could have bought Luxembourg. Of course, that would mean moving to Luxembourg.

Q. It doesn't sound as if you're the right angel for the job.

A. Nobody is. The fellow who had the job before me just up and quit one day. He said that trying to keep politicians on the straight and narrow was harder than herding cats, just not as much fun.

Q. One last question—How do you feel about the Electoral College?

A. You're asking the wrong guy. I never even made it out of high school.

CHAPTER VIII

THE ANGEL FAYE

WHEN I LOOKED AROUND, trying to decide which angel I would approach next, my decision was made for me because in a far corner, a female angel was doubled over in laughter. She looked like she was about to topple off her chair, and I must confess I was very curious about what made angels laugh.

Q. Pardon me, but I was wondering if I could ask you a few questions.

As she was still struggling for breath, the best she could do was wave her hand, inviting me to take a seat. I sat and waited her out. It took a couple of minutes, but she was finally able to speak.

A. What did you want to know?

Q. Well, for openers, I'm dying to know what you're laughing at.

She showed me the magazine she had been reading.

Q. TV Guide?!

A. It's my Bible. Whoops, I hope you understand that's just a figure of speech.

Q. Of course. You must really enjoy the articles. I never realized they were so funny.

A. I don't read the articles. I read the listings.

Q. They're funny?

A. Not all of them, but when I read the little blurbs, they remind me of the episode. Like I was just reading about this episode of *Frasier*, the one where Niles winds up setting fire to Frasier's favorite couch.

Q. You've memorized every episode of *Frasier*?

A. I've memorized every episode of every show.

Q. Wow.

A. Yes, I believe that television is the greatest invention of all time. That's why I'm so proud to be associated with it.

Q. A lot of people regard TV as a terrible waste of time.

A. Well, I happen to regard a lot of people as a terrible waste of time.

Q. I never imagined they'd even have TV in Heaven.

A. It wouldn't be Heaven without it. The only problem is that some angels don't feel that way, so I often have to mute it.

Q. That must make it hard on you.

A. Fortunately, I can read lips. Besides, they're mostly re-runs, so I've seen them before.

Q. How many times have you seen that *Frasier* you were reading about?

A. Roughly four hundred times. But it just keeps getting better and better. I guess that's because I'm getting to know the characters so well. I think I love Roz best of all.

Q. Do you have a favorite show?

A. Wouldn't that be like asking a mother if she has a favorite child? Each in its own way is special. But just between us, I must confess I have a special soft spot for quiz shows.

Q. That's interesting. Why do you think that is?

A. I believe it must be because they're so educational.

Q. There are those who believe that TV destroys brain cells.

A. I wouldn't want to sound judgmental, but some people don't have two brain cells to rub together, if you ask me.

Q. What are some of the things you've learned recently?

A. Well, I've learned that Grenada was the first horse to win the Belmont Stakes in 1880 in the time of two minutes, 47 seconds; that Venus's rotation is retrograde, meaning it spins in the opposite direction to the other planets; that the three major resources of Jordan are phosphates, potash and shale oil; that Mount Everest is exactly 29,028 feet high, though you'd think if it snowed a lot some week, it might make it to 29,029 feet or even 29,030 feet

I felt I had to make my escape before my head exploded, but I guess I shouldn't have said anything, even if I was muttering under my breath.

A. That's not very nice, young man. I told you I could read lips.

Q. I'm sorry. I really do apologize.

A. Lip reading, otherwise known as speech reading, is the process by which…

With a sniff of disgruntlement, Faye returned to her magazine. As I made my escape, I could hear her cackle follow me like an ill-wind.

CHAPTER IX

THE ANGEL LUCAS

AS I PUT AS MUCH DISTANCE between me and Faye as possible, I spied a very short angel whose head barely cleared the top of the table at which he pored over what I discovered was a crossword puzzle. As I slid into a chair across from him, I thought he was so engrossed, he hadn't even noticed me. But he had.

A. You wouldn't happen to know a 17-letter word for an anvil, would you?

Q. I'm afraid not.

A. I didn't expect you to.

Q. If I may be so bold, you seem to be rather dispirited.

A. Certainly discouraged.

Q. It's not just the crossword puzzle, is it?

A. Hardly. The cause of my lethargy is that, for all intents and purposes, I've been out of work for over sixty years.

Q. That is a problem. What is it you do, or did?

A. My job was guiding genius. Hence, I've been unemployed since April 18,1955.

Q. What happened on that date?

A. Einstein died.

Q. And you're telling me there are no geniuses left?

A. Nothing much to speak of.

Q. I find that hard to believe.

A. Of course you do. That's because human beings throw the word around as recklessly as rice at a wedding. By actual count, in the history of the world, there have been nine geniuses. But if you believe, say, **People** magazine, they are as plentiful as fleas on a bloodhound. Everyone who has ever directed a movie that turned a profit, been the lawyer of a celebrity criminal, made a financial killing on Wall Street, or made the cover of **People**, for that matter, qualifies for their pantheon.

Q. I take it that you've been on a first-name basis with all the biggest brains in history. Is there any one moment that stands out for you?

A. No.

Q. Come on, there must be something. The supper during which Socrates expounded on the nature of truth? The day Shakespeare drafted Hamlet's soliloquy? Isaac Newton's discovery of gravity?

A. What?! You think Newton was one of the nine?

Q. Naturally, I assumed...

A. The man was just lucky he fell asleep under an apple tree. If it had been a palm tree, a coconut could have fallen on his head. Let me tell you, a fellow gets beaned with one of those babies, his big concern isn't with the laws of nature, it's his health insurance.

Q. Still, he did discover gravity.

A. He didn't discover it; all he did was name it. What? Do you really think he was the first person who ever noticed that things didn't fall up?

Q. Okay, who was the greatest genius?

A. That's easy. It was Og.

Q. I never heard of him.

A. Of course you didn't. For one thing, he never made the cover of People. For another, he came along quite a while before your time.

Q. What made him so great?

A. He invented the alphabet.

Q. That is a remarkable achievement.

A. It was even better before he caved in to outside pressure.

Q. What do you mean?

A. He had a wife who thought she was creative. Q, X and Z were her idea.

Q. So Og compromised.

A. It was either that or sleeping outside with the tyrannosaurs. Genius is a demanding mistress, but it's nothing compared to a pushy wife.

Q. Who was the second greatest?

A. That would be Charles of the Ritz.

Q. Just because he burned the cheese a little bit?

A. Nah, that was just a happy accident. What made Charles a genius is that he got away with charging $25 for a burned cheese sandwich.

Q. Is there nobody these days who shows even a spark of genius?

A. The pickings are awfully slim, but I suppose if I had to come up with one name, it would be Oprah.

Q. Oprah Winfrey is a genius?

A. I put it to you that turning lead into gold used to be considered a pretty big deal. But this woman has managed to turn drivel into two billion dollars. I think even Og would have been impressed.

CHAPTER X

THE ANGEL CYRUS

MY NEXT SUBJECT was an unlikely looking angel. He appeared listless and slightly befuddled—like someone who'd just been stuck in an elevator between floors or been trapped at a Pauly Shore movie marathon.

He sat, half-dozing, at the far corner of the bar. Gabriel was talking to him as I approached. "Believe me," Gabriel was saying, "it's not my idea. I hate travel. It's the little woman. She wants to be in Fiji on the 24th, in L.A. for her bridge tournament on the 26th and in London, in time for Wimbledon, on the 27th. Is it possible?"

"I'll see what I can do," the sleepy angel yawned.

On the floor at his feet, I noticed a pair of battered old suitcases sporting decals and stickers that read, "Cleveland—the 8th Wonder of the World," "I Got My Clams Steamed in Pismo Beach," "I (Heart) Minsk," and one that, faded though it was, made the hairs stand up on the back of my neck—"Visit Giza, Future Home of the Pyramids."

As Gabriel moved off, I moved in, sliding on to the adjoining stool.

Q. Hello. What's your name?

A. Cyrus.

Q. And you've got something to do with travel?

A. I've got everything to do with it. And, believe me, it's not easy, what with all the different time zones. Half the time, I don't know if I'm coming or going.

Q. You travel by plane?

A. No, shooting stars. Clouds used to be the best way to fly. Slow. Stress-free. You could really stretch out. You could read all the way. One trip, I read all of Mark Twain and got halfway through Proust.

Q. So you miss the old days?

A. Sure do. If only we could turn the clock back. There were relaxing carriage rides, train trips, long sea voyages and, on occasion, an exhilarating gallop across the meadow. Once in a great while, for a refreshing change of scenery, ascent in a hot air balloon. Today, I get hit with so many rush jobs, it's all about speed.

Q. What do you do for relaxation?

A. Mainly, to unwind, I go rainbow sliding.

Q. What's that like?

A. They're like those waterslides at the theme parks, except we don't have to buy tickets or stand in line all day.

Rainbow memories brought a momentary sparkle to his eyes, but once again his head began to nod. Before he could doze off, I asked him what his duties now entailed.

As quickly as the years had taken wing from his weary brow, they returned with a vengeance. It was like speed-reading *The Picture of Dorian Gray*.

A. Cars and buses, jet planes and helicopters, motorcycles and rollerblades. And, as if all that weren't awful enough, cigarette boats, parachutes and bungee cords! It's all madness. The trip, itself, used to be part and parcel of the travel experience. People used to voyage and journey. The very words, themselves, suggest an experience of self-discovery. People set sail, they cast off, they even sallied forth. Now, the whole point is to cheat death. These days, people's idea of a trip is a ride at some loathsome carnival that combines the worst elements of speed, noise and weightlessness. Today, travel is strictly a matter of moving from point A to point B and back to point A in as pointless a way as is mechanically possible. If someone ever devises a way to transport human beings through pneumatic tubes, he'll make a fortune.

Q. It does sound like you have your hands full. What do you consider the single biggest problem with air travel?

A. Leg-room. People keep getting taller and seats keep getting smaller.

Q. Do you see a solution?

A. Oh, sure, but it'll mean first soaking passengers in olive oil.

Q. I don't know if this falls under the category of travel, but I am curious about one thing.

A. Don't ask! I still don't understand how frequent flyer miles work.

Q. That's not it. Why is it, if travel is so much bother, people still insist on taking trips?

A. I, myself, blame it on the movies.

Q. I don't see the connection.

A. In the movies, they don't show you any of the bad or boring parts of travel. People in movies never spend six hours going through customs. And they're never strip-searched because they look a tiny bit like a fugitive terrorist. In the movies, people never get sick from the water. Their hotel rooms are always ready and waiting and the telephone always works. In the movies, people spend all their time falling in love, not trying to track down their lost luggage. The clincher, though, is that in the movies, people can spend their entire holidays in Rome, eating pasta and drinking wine, and never gain an ounce. When you get right down to it, the worst thing that ever happens to tourists in the movies is that they'd be seduced by Rosanno Brazzi.

Q. Now that you mention it, he did pop up in an awful lot of those movies.

A. The man did more for the travel industry than honey-roasted peanuts and Dramamine combined.

Q. There have been a number of people who helped revolutionize travel over the years. Is there any one person whose contribution seems greater than all the rest?

A. Absolutely.

Q. Henry Ford? The Wright brothers?

A. H.G. Wells.

Q. Why H.G. Wells? What did he do for travel?

A. He dreamed up the time machine. The person sat at home in a chair and time did all the traveling. It was a brainstorm. You wanted to go somewhere, you flipped a dial and it came to you. Next best was Gutenberg.

Q. The Gutenberg who invented the printing press?

A. There was another Gutenberg?

Q. But, what's the printing press got to do with travel?

A. After Gutenberg, if people suddenly decided they wanted to go visit Timbuktu, they could read about it first. After twenty pages, you got bored, you could put the book down and you were home. No packing, no catching the next plane out, no worrying about the tse-tse flies.

Q. Some people say travel is broadening.

A. Sure, and some people are cannibals; there's no accounting for taste. As someone once pointed out, if travel were all that broadening, stewardesses and Buzz Aldrin would be the smartest people on earth.

CHAPTER XI

THE ANGEL LYDIA

THE LADY WHO NOW SAT across from me was of indeterminate age. She didn't appear to be either young or old, but she could have been anything in between. Her hair hung down in soft curls and she smelled of lavender. She created a slight breeze with a beautiful fan. She gazed at me over it, like Scarlett checking out the ballroom at Tara. She might have just stepped out of one of those expensive greeting cards—the oversized ones with the padded hearts on the front, that you give your wife when you've forgotten her birthday or the day after you've made a fool of yourself at the office Christmas party.

She wasn't exactly beautiful, but she definitely had an air about her. But, that might have been the lavender.

By now, I knew better than to go by appearances where these angels were concerned. Looking at her soft, moist lips and those large, limpid eyes, I was pretty darn sure she had nothing to do with love and romance. She was probably the angel in charge of slot machines and the numbers racket, I was thinking. Just to break the ice, I hazarded a guess. "You have anything to do with professional wrestlers or longshoremen?"

A. Not directly, but nobody, I dare say, is immune to my influence.

Q. Really?

A. Oh, yes. You see, I'm Lydia, the angel of romance.

Q. Well, what do you know. It just goes to show that some-times you *can* judge a book by its cover. But maybe only when it's a romance novel.

A. At least romance used to be my field. Now, of course, the field has faded away like an old rose pressed between the pages of a diary. It's really so sad. *Quel tristesse*. In olden days, romance meant a lover scaling walls, slaying dragons of one sort or another, and pledging himself to true love.

Q. Are you talking about chivalry? Don't you think that's pretty outdated stuff?

A. And just what, sir, is outdated about eternal bliss? What's unfashionable about lovers pledging their troth to one another?

Q. Their what?

A. That's another thing - people used to know what troth meant. Now, their lawyers hammer out pre-nuptials. Once upon a time, we had soul-mates and two hearts that beat as one. Now, they're significant others. Now, men snigger about hooters, and women giggle about butts.

How can romance flourish when you treat one another like so many interchangeable body parts, like Chevys or the Colonel's chicken?

Q. Who do you regard as the greatest romantics?

A. One who readily comes to mind is Shah Jahan. He's the man who built the Taj Mahal as a mausoleum when his wife, the lovely Mumtaz Mahall, passed away.

Q. The Taj Mahal was a heck of a gesture, okay.

A. But, nothing compared to the Taj Shirley.

Q. The Taj Shirley? I'm afraid I've never heard of it.

A. It was the house Shah Jahan had to build for his second wife, once she got a gander at the tomb he'd built for number one. As Shirley put it, and rightly so if you want my opinion, "That woman's living better than me, and she's dead!"

Q. The place must have been spectacular.

A. Oh, my, yes. Not only was it twice as big as the Taj Mahal, but the reflecting lake was indoors. Say what you will about Shirley, she definitely knew what she wanted.

Q. Who else comes to mind when you think of the great romantics?

A. Norman Kuperman ranks right up there near the top.

Q. What did he do?

A. It's what he didn't do. During World War II, PFC Kuperman got to meet Marlene Dietrich at the Hollywood Canteen. She kissed him on the cheek, and he never again washed his face. Now, that's what I call romantic.

Q. It's not very hygienic.

A. That's true, but I should remind you that romance isn't for sissies. Look at Van Gogh. For love, he gave up an ear. And Edward, you may recall, even gave up the throne of England. If it doesn't involve enormous sacrifice, it isn't romance, dear boy, it's just dating.

Q. I notice that you haven't mentioned any women. Aren't any of them romantic?

A. Any of them? All of them are romantic. What else but romance would blind them to reality to such a degree that they would agree to marry you men?

Q. And just what's so terrible about men?

I must admit that her response caught me completely by surprise. She laughed. She just threw her head back and howled. It was a good ten minutes before she even began to recover. She started wiping her eyes with a handkerchief. Every few seconds, she would start to speak, but she'd be overcome by a new wave of giggles.

She finally got control, smiled, sighed softly, and said, "Well, dear heart, there you have it. For all the obvious faults and dreadful shortcomings of your gender, you men do make us laugh so. In a world without men, women might never laugh again. Or cry, I suppose."

Q. I must say, for someone in the love game, you don't seem to have your heart in it. Don't you believe in your own product?

A. Of course I do, but you people are hopeless. Lust has long replaced love as the governing emotion, and romance has given way to pornography. Why wouldn't I be a pessimist? Once upon a time, I truly believed the world sought what I had to offer. But, the scales fell from my eyes, and I then saw the tunnel at the end of the light.

Q. Is there nothing that can be done?

A. I can't speak for everyone, but I manage to get by, renting *Casablanca* and *Now, Voyager* every few months. And a little white wine never hurts.

CHAPTER XII

THE ANGEL MORRIS

THE LAVENDER LINGERED ON, but the person who now sat facing me couldn't have been less like Miss Lydia. He was bald, getting on in years, thirty pounds overweight and, peering out from behind thick bifocals, looked as if befuddled might have been his middle name. He was drinking a Dr. Brown's celery tonic out of the bottle, and he wore a Brooklyn Dodgers baseball cap. I don't know where I would have pigeonholed Morris, but I certainly didn't imagine his bailiwick to be technology. But, that's what he told me.

Q. I guess you are one happy angel.

A. Oh? And why's that? Do you know something I don't?

Q. I just meant that, although romance and the arts might be going to the dogs, you can't knock modern technology.

A. No, you can't, if you're smart. It could knock back and really hurt you.

Q. You're not a fan of progress?

A. I'll give you progress! Do you realize that they now have a lethal gas you can't see or smell? With just two ounces of it, you could wipe Southern California off the map. I see you're smiling.

Q. Just visualizing.

A. Be that as it may, Mr. Wisenheimer, my point is that one man's progress is another man's poison gas. And a very good point it is.

Q. When did you first sour on your job?

A. It was a pretty gradual thing. Way back when, I wouldn't have traded places with anyone. I'll never forget the day the wheel was invented. There was such excitement!

Q. Did they have any idea what to do with it?

A. None whatsoever! That's what made it so exciting. Everyone sensed that they were on to something big, but they had no idea what.

Q. Was it one person who made the discovery?

A. Of course. It's always one person. As soon as you get a second person in the room, all he'll do is tell the first person to stop horsing around and get a real job.

Q. So, who was it who discovered the wheel?

A. It was a guy named Benny, he was just fooling around one day with different shapes. It's very fortunate he finally came up with round.

Q. What do you mean?

A. For the longest time, he got hung up on triangles. Imagine driving on four steel- rimmed triangles!

Q. When did things start going downhill for you?

A. After Edison, I'd have to say it stopped being fun.

Q. You admired Edison?

A. He flabbergasted me. He had a brain on him the size of a bowling ball. They say that the legs are the first thing to go, but if you've got a brain like Edison's, it's the neck. A head that size, you expect to see four guys named Lars climbing up and planting a flag.

Q. Which of all the inventions has impressed you the most?

A. Where to start? There were so many, you couldn't count. The safety pin was a doozy. Very simple, but a real money maker. And baseball cleats were another. Without the cleats, nobody would have ever gotten to first base. Halfway there, they'd fall down. It's a very slippery game, baseball. Without the cleats, it would have been ice skating. The escalator was another snappy idea. And the juicer's a pip. Nothing I enjoy better in the morning than a nice fresh glass of orange juice. You like orange juice?

Q. Sure.

A. Everybody does, but do you ever go to a park and see a statue of the smart guy who made it all possible? And what about the fellow who invented popcorn?!

Q. Funny, I never thought of popcorn being an invention.

A. Well, it doesn't exactly grow on trees. But, technically speaking, you're right. Popcorn's always been around. But, for the longest time, it wasn't food, it was packing material.

In fact, it was a guy with a warehouse full of the stuff who changed things all around. One night, he sat up in bed and shouted, "Butter and salt!" Scared his wife half to death, but he made millions. And that's where we got the saying, "One man's packing material is another man's snack."

Q. Do you have faith in the future?

A. Of course. Why wouldn't I?

Q. Well, sometimes I worry that technology is moving too fast for us. I worry that machines will do away with us.

A. No matter how big the machinery, no matter how intelligent or how powerful, that will never happen! At least not so long as we remember one thing.

Q. And is that the fact that we were created in God's image and that there is a spark of immortality in each of us?

A. No. The thing we mustn't ever forget is to always include an off-switch.

CHAPTER XIII

THE ANGEL DOROTHY

ACROSS THE ROOM, sitting quietly, knitting, was a plump little lady who resembled Aunt Bea in the old *Andy Griffith Show*. She looked content. More than content, she looked serene. Maybe the word I'm hunting for is angelic. I wondered if she might be slightly feebleminded. Ignorance, I've often found, is its own reward. It helps people sleep at night, avoid worry lines, and somehow sit through and, yes, even enjoy the likes of Fox sitcoms, Ben Stiller movies and revivals of *Cats*. Judging by the beatific smile on this one's face, I would have taken her for one of those truly extreme cases—the sort who actually look forward to PBS pledge nights.

"Finally," I said by way of breaking the ice, "a cheerful angel."

"Oh, indeed I am. Do you suppose that's because I only deal indirectly with people?"

"I'm sure I wouldn't know," I said, trying not to take her remark personally. "Who do you deal with?"

A. Why, dogs, of course.

Q. Dogs?!

A. Of course. Why do you sound so surprised?

Q. Well, I just never imagined that poodles would have their own angel.

A. Isn't that just like a human being to imagine that heaven would be more concerned with them than with their pets!

Q. But, they're just poor, dumb, creatures.

A. Of course, dear. That's why we always try to make allowances for people.

Q. I was referring to the dogs!

A. I know.

Q. Dogs are swell, but how much real satisfaction can there be in overseeing the affairs of creatures who pee on trees and go bow-wow?

A. And who are fearless, loving, gentle and loyal? Who don't start wars, lie, cheat or betray their friends? Whose simple goodness and piety serve as an example to the saints?

And, yet, here you sit, truly astonished that dogs hold a special place in all our hearts. Now, that's what I call astonishing. It may further shock you to learn that their place in heaven is secure, while the human race is definitely skating on very thin ice.

Q. I never imagined.

A. Of course you didn't. That's because it's not their way to brag. Even here on earth, when a dog wins a race or a blue ribbon, he never hogs the spotlight. He's always more than willing to share the glory with his people.

Q. You don't have to sell me. I like dogs as much as anyone.

A. I should hope so. I probably shouldn't tell tales out of school, but the possibility of pulling the plug on the human race has been discussed more than once.

Q. No!

A. Yes! Those in favor of the idea argued that it would be far more merciful in the long run, considering the harm you were doing to the planet and all its other inhabitants. The only thing that prevented the motion from coming to a final vote was that the dogs went to bat for you. Don't ask me why, but they definitely have a soft spot in their hearts for people. It may sound like just so much bow-wow to you, sir, but it was only their eloquence that saved your bacon.

Q. Gee.

A. Gee, indeed. It turns out that the only thing the dogs can't figure out is why on earth, if they're your best friends, the way you're always claiming, so many of you insist on chumming around with cats.

Q. Don't look at me. I'm allergic. Tell me, are all the other animals in Heaven, too?

A. Just like with people, some are, some aren't.

Q. Which ones aren't?

A. The bad ones, of course. Just like with people. We do have a saying, though, that it's easier for a rich man to pass through the eye of a needle than for a camel to enter the Kingdom of God. Nasty things, always spitting.

Q. Miss Dorothy?

A. Yes?

Q. I was just wondering...you wouldn't happen to know a little schnauzer named Whiskers, would you?

A. Oh, indeed I do. It took me weeks to heaven-break that little dickens, but it was worth it. He's a love.

Q. Would you tell him I said, hello?

A. My pleasure.

CHAPTER XIV

THE ANGELS
GEORGE AND JANET

TWO ANGELS JOINED ME in the booth. They were a middle-aged couple who gave the impression that they were bone-weary. They were George and Janet, and they seemed to sigh a lot.

Q. Just what is it that you do?

A. (Janet) We oversee parenting. (George) Don't blame us. God knows we've tried. (Janet) There, there, dear, I'm sure the nice gentleman realizes we do the best we can. (George) More's the pity.

Tears began rolling down their cheeks. They made little sobbing noises in unison. I don't mind telling you, my heart went out to them.

Q. Why are you being so hard on yourselves?

A. (Janet) Please excuse us. It's just that when we started out, we had such high hopes for the future. (George) We were so young. (Janet) We were idealists. We actually believed that there could be such things as perfect, nurturing, parents. (George) And don't forget those wonderful, loving, tots. We believed in them, too! Oh, where did we go wrong? How could we have been so blind? (Janet) It wasn't our fault, George. You mustn't blame yourself for the failings of others. (George) But it all happened under our watch. (Janet) We're only angels, dear. Who were we to compete with Dr. Spock and all those other child-rearing experts with their best-selling books and their newspaper columns and their appearances on the *Today Show*?

Q. I still don't know why you're so upset.

A. (George) Of course not. But, then, I wager you don't have children. (Janet) You don't, do you, dear?

Q. How can you tell?

A. (George) Easy. No tics, no worry lines, most of your hair intact. (Janet) It's the eyes, George. They're the giveaway. Tiny mirrors to the soul.

Q. And just what do you see in my eyes?

A. (Janet) Your soul. It's still there. (George) Our big mistake was in letting parents keep their children around even after the children are bigger than they are. It breaks down the natural order of things when the parent gives a command and the child says, "Oh, yeah?" or "Who's going to make me?" or, worst of all, "You and who else?'"

Q. It sounds like you're talking about teenagers.

A. (Janet) Ooh, the awful "T" word. We try not to say it. (George) It's a modern aberration, you know. Both the word and the thing itself.

Q. But, haven't we always had teenagers?

A. (Janet) Of course not.

Q. But, how could it be avoided?

A. (Janet) In those happier days, there was simply no such thing as a teenager. (George) You went straight from being an adorable little six-year-old to being a very short coal miner.

Q. Surely you don't think life was better back in those dark ages, do you?

A. (Janet) It was if you were a parent. You're too young to remember, I suppose, but there was a time when youngsters were grateful if they found an apple in their Christmas stocking. (George) I should say so. They were grateful for the stocking. It was the thought that counted.

Q. When would you say that things started falling apart?

A. (George) When parents started letting their children have spending money. (Janet) And the car keys. (George) Cable. (Janet) Store-bought clothes. (George) Their own

TVs. (Janet) Their own phones. (George) Their own opinions. (Janet) Their own bathrooms.

Q. Their own bathrooms?

A. (George) One thing leads to another.

Q. Why do you think people persist in having children?

A. (Janet) Hope springs eternal? (George) Bad habits die hard? (Janet) Preservation of the species? (George) For their pelts?

CHAPTER XV

THE ANGEL SEBASTIAN

NEXT UP WAS A STUDIOUS-LOOKING fellow who wore horned-rim glasses, a vest complete with watch fob, and spats. He puffed on a cigar. He looked at me as I approached, shook his bearded head and smiled in a way I didn't like.

A. A bed-wetter, if I'm not mistaken.

Q. If you're referring to me, you're very much mistaken.

A. That's what they all say.

Q. Who are you, anyway?

A. I'm Sebastian, the angel of psychiatry.

Q. What do you do beside insult people you don't know?

A. No insult intended. Some of the greatest men in history have been bed-wetters.

Q. Name two.

A. I can't even name one. No bed-wetter has ever achieved greatness. The only thing they've ever achieved is a damp mattress. I just said that so you wouldn't feel so embarrassed about that nasty habit.

Q. Thanks a lot. What exactly is your mission?

A. I told you, I'm in charge of psychiatry.

Q. What does that consist of?

A. I try to keep people like Dr. Phil from getting too big a head, reminding the Johnny-Come-Latelies that they didn't invent it.

Q. Because Sigmund Freud did.

A. Don't make me laugh. Sigmund Freud was a classic bed-wetter. The only thing he did was give names to the things the ancient Greeks had been writing dirty plays about.

Q. You mean the id, the ego and the super ego?

A. Right. Once Freud named them, people got the idea they could be cured of their craziness. Fat chance.

Q. So you're saying Freud was a fake?

A. Of course, they're all fakes. But at least Freud had the gimmick.

Q. What gimmick?

A. He was the one who convinced people that he could actually cure what ailed them. Before he came along, people assumed they were miserable because they were slaves or peasants, poor, ugly, unhappily married, unhappily unmarried, cripples or hungry. All very good reasons to be unhappy, I would point out. But Freud convinced them it was because they all wanted to sleep with their mothers just because he wanted to sleep with his. The man was a mess. It figures he'd concentrate on dreams, especially wet ones.

Q. As I understand it, he felt dreams were the most direct route to the sub-conscious.

A. Nonsense. It just gave people something to talk about. In the beginning, his clients would just sit there like mummies, staring at him for fifty minutes. People didn't think it was right to be charged for sitting and staring. Freud understood that if he didn't come up with something, he'd actually have to go out and find a job. So he came up with dreams. Everybody likes talking about their dreams. Makes them feel special. Some people discovered they didn't dream or, if they did, couldn't remember them. So they'd make things up. It beat just sitting and staring.

Q. So you think Freud was just a charlatan?

A. Of course, but even I have to give him credit for bringing the couch in from the living room. That was a stroke of genius.

Q. Why do you consider that such a big deal?

A. By turning it from furniture into office equipment, he made it tax-deductible.

Chapter XVI

The Angels Julie and Jud

WHEN THE NEXT PAIR OF ANGELS took their place before me, I looked around and realized they were the last angels left. I tried to guess what their roles might be. What could possibly be left? Angels of medical malpractice or insurance adjustors? Angels of small household appliances? In the end, was I to discover that, not only did Cocker Spaniels and Chihuahuas have a higher standing in heaven than we do, but so did electric blankets and toaster ovens?

The waiter, who looked totally bushed, wandered over to take last orders. He seemed greatly relieved when the couple waved him off.

Perhaps I should have guessed, but it was getting late and I'd had quite an evening, so I was genuinely taken aback when Julie and Jud told me that their particular arena was religion.

I'm sure you're all saying you would have guessed. Yeah, right. Have it your way. I'm sure you all had Dorothy spotted right off as the dog angel, too.

Q. How have your duties changed over the years?

A. (Julie) We've certainly had to adapt. (Jud) To go with the flow, as it were. Along the way, we had to expand into philosophy, mythology, dietary law. (Julie) And don't forget military strategy and medieval tortures. (Jud) Yes, it's definitely been a broadening experience.

Q. How has religion changed?

A. (Julie) In the old days, there were just a few religions. Nothing too fancy. (Jud) Truth is, if all services had been conducted in Latin, and you closed your eyes, you wouldn't have known where you were. (Julie) But, you know how people are.

Q. Complicated?

A: (Julie) Let's just say, not too bright. So, before you could say Moses in the bulrushes, there were more religions, cults, sects and covens, than you could shake a stick at. (Jud) Tempted as you might be! (Julie) They sprang up like toadstools. Seemed like every time you turned around, someone was speaking in tongues or channeling, reading backwards or twirling in circles. (Jud) Or playing with snakes.

Q. What is religion like in Heaven? I mean, do you all go to church and does God give sermons?

A. (Julie) Of course not.

Q. Why not?

A.(Julie) Because we don't need it. The main point of religion is to remind people that God exists, and He has
rules. Well, up there, where we're the tenants and He's the
landlord, we hardly need reminding that He exists. (Jud)
And if you do need any reminding, just try playing your
stereo after midnight

Q. If you could tell people one thing, what would it be?

A. (Julie) They should keep in mind that, although God
answers all prayers, sometimes they have to accept that
His answer is "no". (Jud) The only thing wrong with people is they keep asking questions long after they've been
provided with all the answers they'll ever need.

Q. You mean the Ten Commandments?

A. (Jud) Of course, that and the Golden Rule. (Julie) The
trouble with most people, if you ask me, is that they seem
to think there are three Commandments and seven Sug-
gestions.

By now, dawn was just coming up. Gabriel was going through the motions of swabbing down the bar top.
All the other angels had wandered off into the night. The
waiter was leaning against the hat rack, no doubt wondering if he'd ever get to go home. I was beginning to feel a
little guilty, but there was still one last question I had to
ask.

Q. Jud, Julie, there is one more thing I just have to know.

They exchanged knowing looks.

A. (Jud) Of course. (Julie) You wouldn't be human if you didn't ask.

Q. God...what is He like?

A. (Julie) The waiter.

Q. God looks like the waiter?

A. (Jud) God is the waiter.

Q. God is the waiter?! Come on, I didn't just fall off the turnip truck.

A. (Jud) Suit yourself, but it's the truth. (Julie) If you don't believe us, ask Him.

Q. He's God and I'm a monkey's uncle.

A. (Jud) Close enough. (Julie) Time we called it a night.

CHAPTER XVII

CLOSING THE JOINT

I DAWDLED. As stupid as it sounded, I couldn't resist. After all, I buy a lottery ticket every week even though I don't have one chance in ten million of winning. What could it hurt on a night I'd already met angels, to ask a middle-aged waiter if he was God. Hell, I've yet to meet a waiter in a Jewish deli who wasn't convinced he was, so what did I have to lose?

I got up, stretched, and walked nonchalantly over to the man by the hat rack.

Q. I don't want to be rude, but those two just told me you were God.

He looked at me as if he were hoping I'd either leave or get to the point.

A. So, what's your question?

Q. My question?! My question is, are you really Him?

A. If by him, you mean me, yes.

Q. I do if you're Him.

A. Well, if I'm not, who is?

Q. So, you really are Him?

A. So help me, me.

Q. Wait a second! You're telling me God is waiting tables in a crummy bar?

A. I've seen worse. In fact, at this very moment, I'm sweeping up a café in downtown Beirut makes this place look like Versailles.

Q. That's not the point. God waiting tables in a bar?! That's outrageous.

A. You're right, I suppose. At my age, it's a little hard on the feet. But, I soak 'em when I get home. Besides, it's honest work, we have a nice clientele and I get Sundays off.

Suddenly, the waiter vanished. A second later, he re-appeared.

Q. What was that all about?

A. Oh, you noticed I left?

Q. Wasn't I supposed to? I mean, it was a darn good trick.

A. I guess I'm just slowing down. Used to be, I really could be everywhere at the same time.

Q. Where were you just then?

A. A giant comet just crashed in Siberia. Comets, volcanoes, tidal waves, I just love that stuff.

Q. What are you doing here at Gabriel's?

A. Mostly, staying in touch with my work force.

Q. You mean like a CEO lunching in the company cafeteria?

A. That's the idea. It shows that you're just one of the guys. It's supposed to boost morale. I'm also in a bowling league. I can't tell you how hard it is for me not to throw strikes. I read all about this stuff in a book about modern management techniques.

Q. Speaking of books, how would you suggest I go about getting this one published? I mean, I heard about all those big shot writers who tried and failed. If Dickens couldn't find a publisher, what chance have I got?

A. Frankly, I wouldn't mind a little positive publicity. Lately, the only time my name gets mentioned in the press is when Time magazine periodically announces my demise or some nutty cult leader claims he's got me on hold.

Q. So what should I do?

A. When you finish the book, give me a holler. I'll make a few calls.

Q. You know people in the book business?

A. I did write a best seller, you know.

Q. I forgot.

A. So did they. I'm still waiting to see my first royalty check. Oh, by the way, your car is working now.

I guess there were a million questions I should have asked, but the old guy looked exhausted, just dying to get home to his Epsom salts.

Q. Well, it's been nice meeting you.

A. Same here.

I paused at the door.

Q. Peace.

A. From your mouth to my ear.

The night was cool and crystal clear. In the sky, I saw a shooting star. I'm sure He did, too. Apparently, He just loves that stuff.

THE END